Kate Leake

WHO ATE THE CAKE?

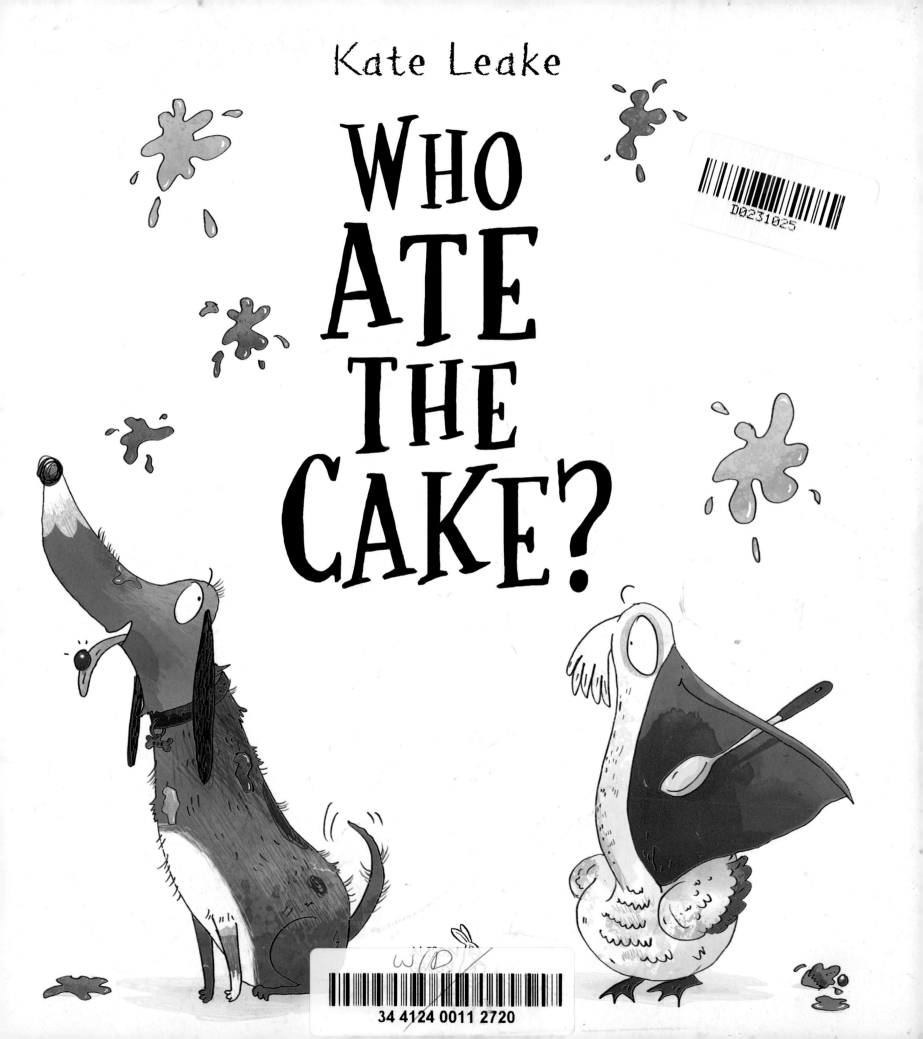

Bob was Freddie's dog.
He was always getting into trouble,
mostly for eating things that he shouldn't.

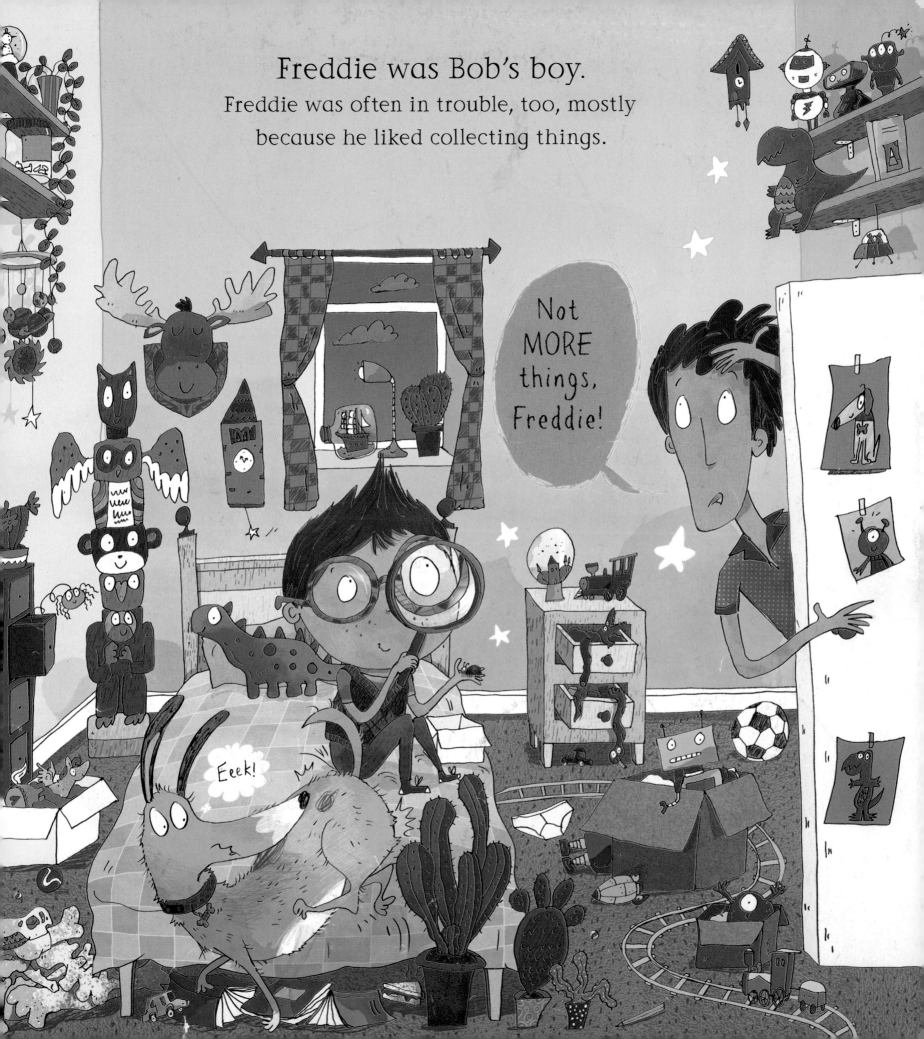

Freddie was Bob's boy.
Freddie was often in trouble, too, mostly
because he liked collecting things.

Every week, Freddie counted up his pocket money, and bought lots of new things from his **Collectors' Weekly** catalogue.
So far, he had collected:

15 Toy cars

11 Comics

12 Robots

7 Cacti

9 Trains

16 Dinosaur bones

5 Ships in bottles

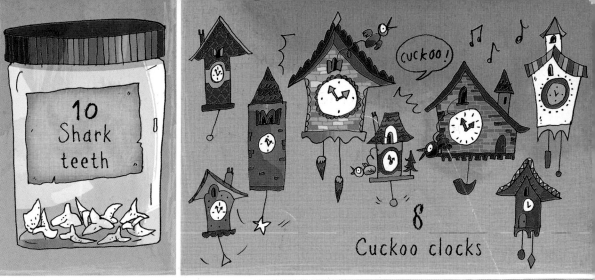

10 Shark teeth

8 Cuckoo clocks

CUCKOO!

6 Snow globes

4 Pink ponies
(which he sent back)

3 Aliens

and a handful of creepy crawlies.

Bob **loved** Freddie's collection. It gave him plenty of interesting things to chew – especially the dinosaur bones.

CRUNCH

Mum and Dad were less happy.
"Freddie!" they said. "There must be
NO more
things!"

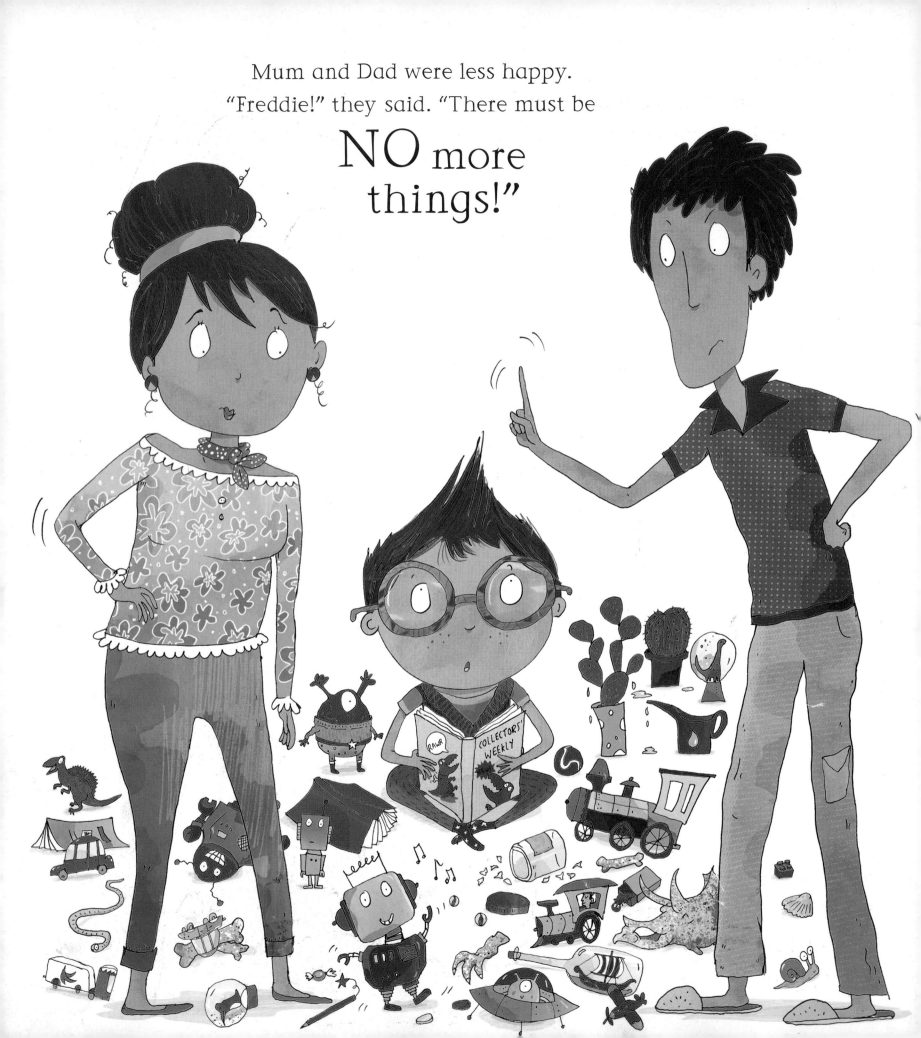

But, that very afternoon,
another huge box arrived. Freddie
had ordered so many things from his
Collectors' Weekly catalogue, that he'd
earned a mystery free gift!

Bob sniffed the box
suspiciously. It smelt
sort of . . . FISHY!

"We'd better not tell Mum and
Dad about this," said Freddie.
Then he lifted the lid and
out popped . . .

Freddie was thrilled.

But Bob didn't like the pelican.
It was **big.**
It was **flappy.**

And its beak was wide enough
to gulp down a computer.

Which is **exactly** what it did,
when Freddie wasn't looking.

"No!" barked Bob.
"Pesky pelican!"

"Shh!" said Freddie. "Mum and Dad mustn't find out about him!"

And that was just the start of the chaos.

First, Mum's knitting went missing.

"Grrr!" growled Bob.
"Pesky pelican!"

Then it was Dad's daffodils.
"Huh?!" gasped Bob. "Pesky pelican!"

DAFFODILS

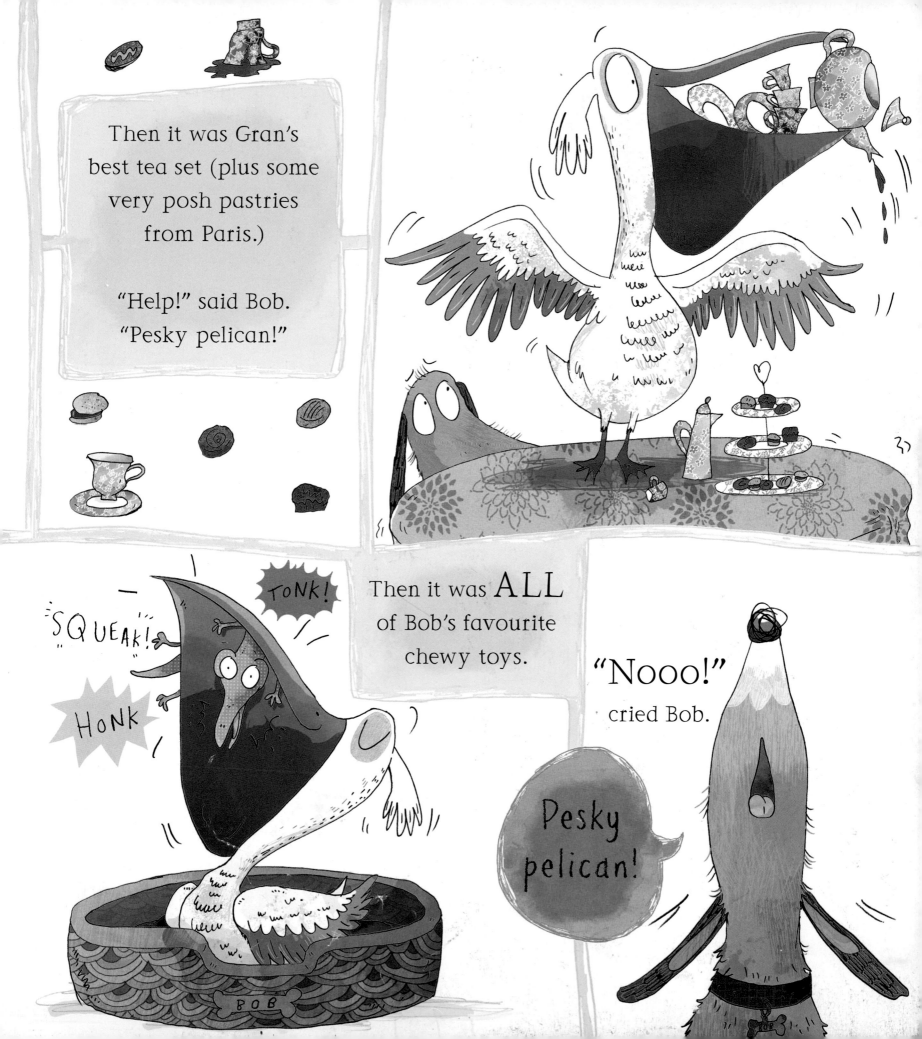

Then it was Gran's best tea set (plus some very posh pastries from Paris.)

"Help!" said Bob. "Pesky pelican!"

Then it was ALL of Bob's favourite chewy toys.

"Nooo!" cried Bob.

Pesky pelican!

SQUEAK!

HONK

TONK!

BOB

But did the pesky pelican get the blame? Of course not.
Nobody knew about *him*. They all blamed Bob instead.

"My knitting!" cried Mum.
"Bad Bob! No biscuit!"

"My daffodils!" groaned Dad.
"Bad Bob! No biscuit!"

"My tea set!" squeaked Gran.
"Bad Bob! No biscuit!"

"My chewy toys!"
howled Bob. "Sad Bob!
More biscuits!"

But nobody understood him.

Bob decided that Pesky Pelican
was nothing but

big bad
beaky

trouble!

But the next day was Freddie's birthday. Bob was determined to be on his best Bob behaviour. That way, he might get a piece of Freddie's Big Birthday Cake.

The cake had been baking all morning, and it smelled SCRUMPTIOUS!

Bob tiptoed into the kitchen to have another good sniff before teatime.

RAWR!

But he was too late!

With one big, beaky GULP, the pelican
ATE THE WHOLE CAKE!
There was nothing left but one
teeny tiny cherry . . .

GULP!

"Noooo!!!"
howled Bob.

"PESKY
PELICAN!!!"

He chased that pesky pelican all round the kitchen
– but the pelican was too fast and flappy for him.

Pans clattered,

plates smashed,

spoons scattered,

food splashed . . .

. . . and everyone came running to see what the commotion was.

"My kitchen!" shrieked Mum.

"My cake!" said Freddie.

"Bad Bob!" shouted everyone.

"Look at this mess!"

There was custard on the windows, plates on the floor, jam on the ceiling and a pelican on the fridge.

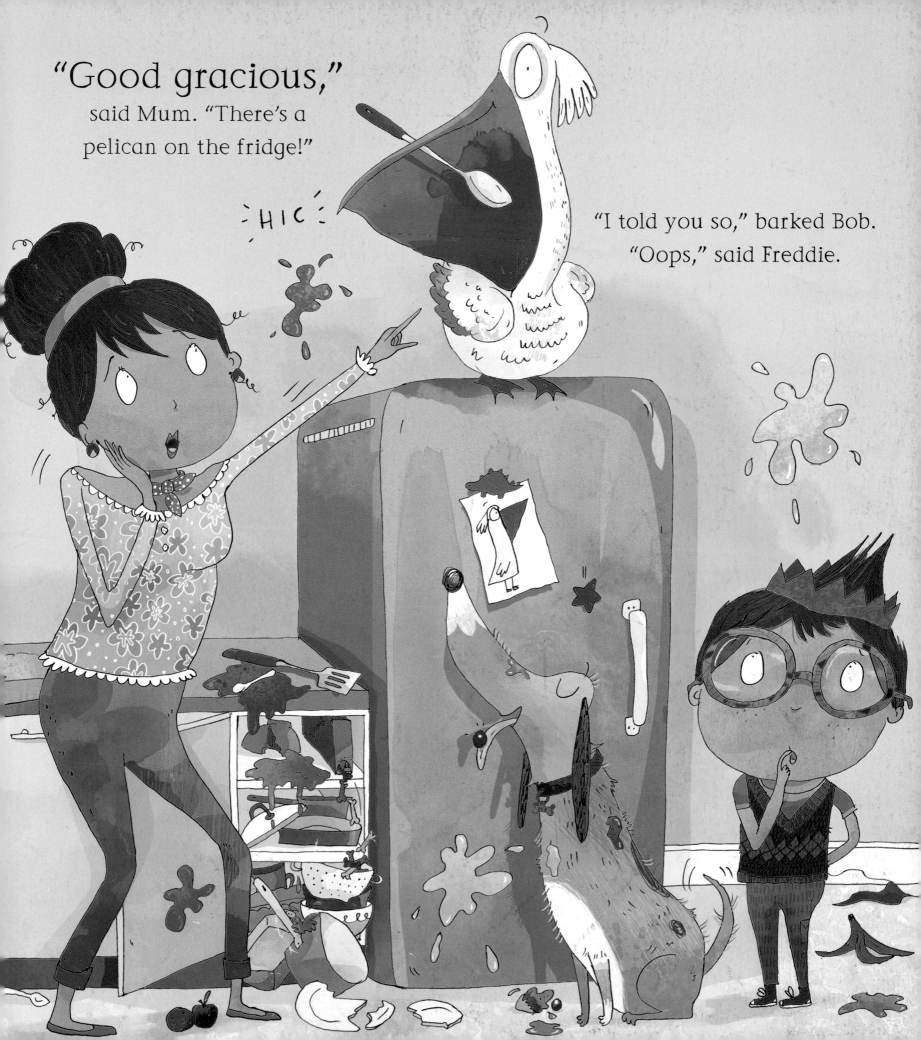

It took a long time to unpack the pelican's beak.
Inside, they found:

One entire Big Birthday Cake,
(minus one teeny tiny cherry),

Gran's tea set

and some very soggy
pastries from Paris,

Dad's daffodils,

something that had
once been Mum's
knitting,

all of Bob's
chewy toys . . .

RAWR!

Tut!

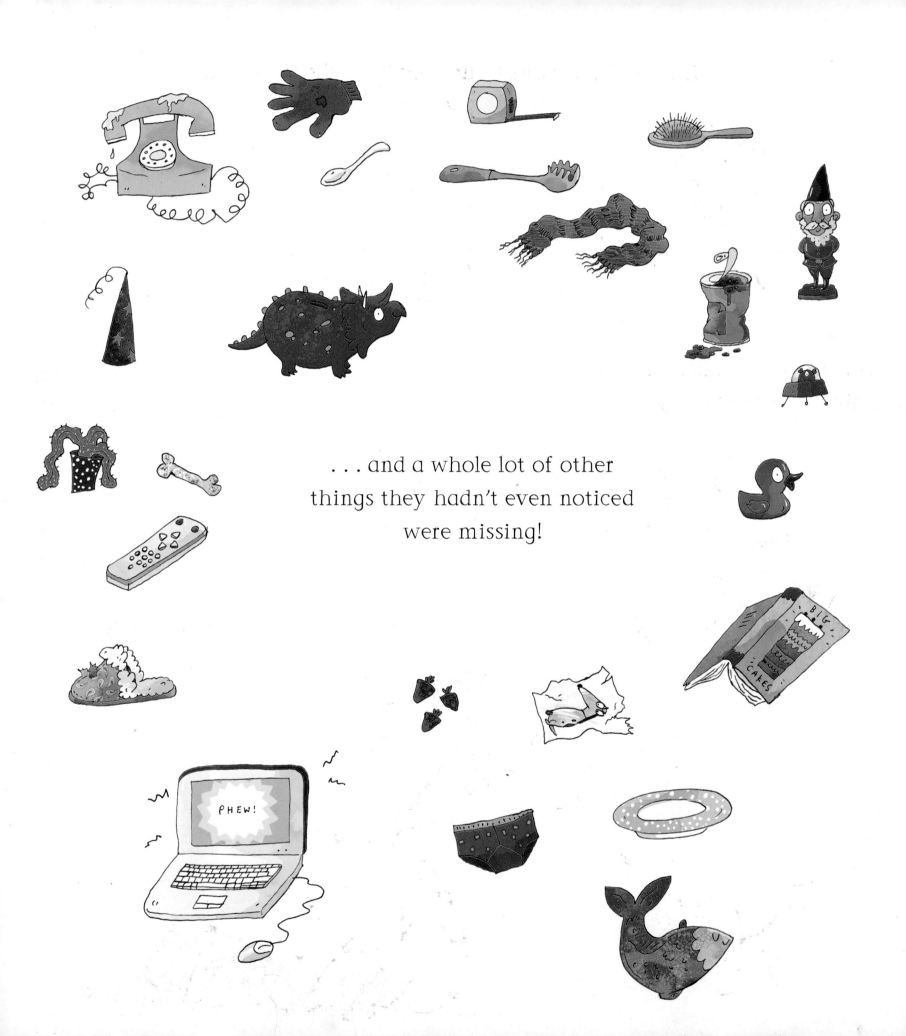

. . . and a whole lot of other
things they hadn't even noticed
were missing!

"Poor Bob!" cried everyone.

All those days of "No biscuit!"
and he'd not been a Bad Bob at all!
"Bob needs a treat!" said Dad. "What
would you like for tea, Bob?"

BISCUITS

BOB

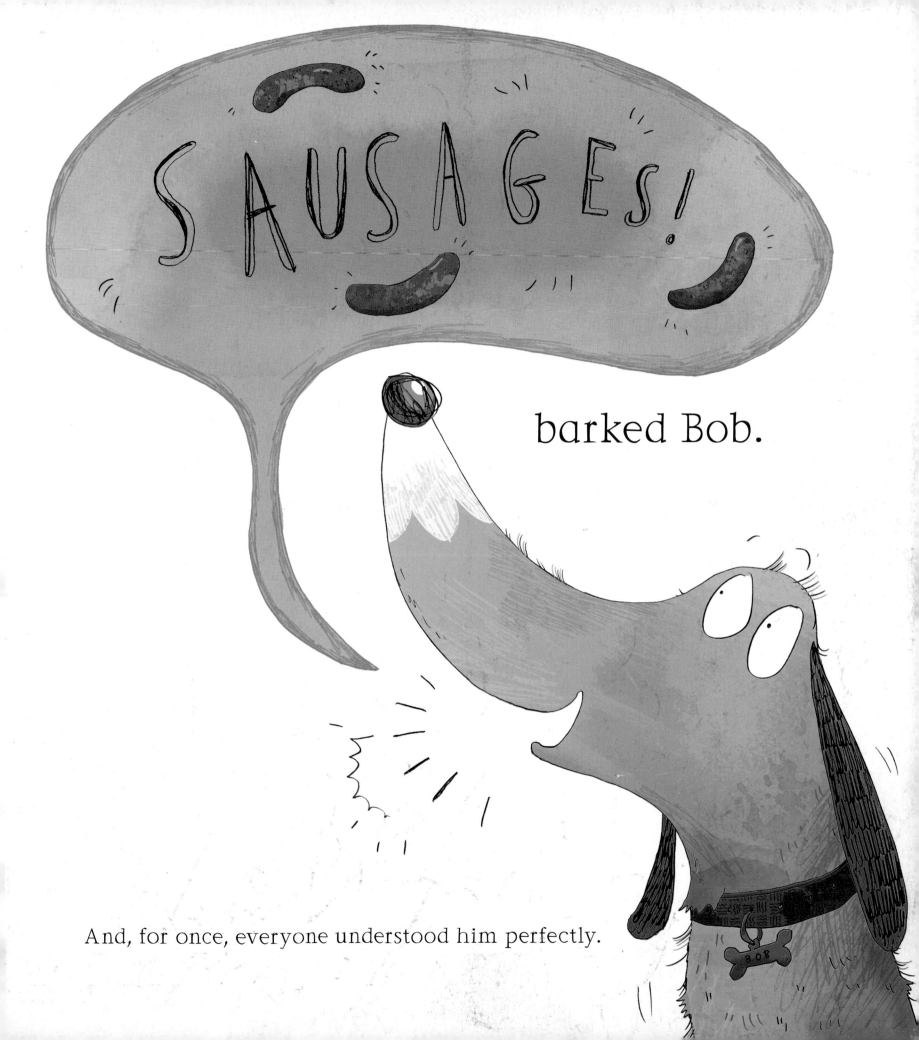

Bob ate a **lot** of sausages,

while Mum and Dad
stuffed that peckish pelican's
beak full of juicy fish,

help!

and Gran and Freddie
baked another cake.

After all the fuss, it had turned into Freddie's
best birthday ever – especially when
there was a knock at the door . . .

. . . and another mystery
gift arrived!

First published in the UK in 2017 by
Alison Green Books
An imprint of Scholastic Children's Books
Euston House, 24 Eversholt Street
London NW1 1DB
A division of Scholastic Ltd
www.scholastic.co.uk
London – New York – Toronto – Sydney – Auckland
Mexico City – New Delhi – Hong Kong

HB ISBN: 978 1 407164 31 1
PB ISBN: 978 1 407164 32 8

For my WONDERFUL Alan,
with all my love xxx